Noah's Floating Animal Park

By Janine Suter

Illustrated by Richard Gunther

For Kellie, Kingsley & Matthew, in memory of your beautiful Dorinda Alice

Original edition copyright © 2008 by Janine Suter
Master Books® first printing: August 2009

ISBN-13: 978-0-89051-576-1
ISBN-10: 0-89051-576-X
Library of Congress Number: 2009929846

Printed in China

Please visit our website for other great titles:
www.masterbooks.net

For information regarding author interviews, please contact the publicity department at 1-870-438-5288.

Master Books®
A Division of New Leaf Publishing Group
www.masterbooks.net

The Bible tells of Noah, a kind and righteous man,
Who had a wife, and three good sons, named Japheth, Shem, and Ham.
Noah and his wife and sons, and all of their wives, too,
Built an ark that was the world's first-ever floating zoo.
This story is not make-believe. It actually occurred.
The whole event got written down, recorded word for word.

Although the world had started well, it was now in trouble.
God knew that something needed to be done right on the double.
Sin was spoiling everything — it was really chilling:
Stealing, fighting, everywhere! And lots and lots of killing.

To make things worse, some sons of God then hatched a wicked plot.
They took some wives and had some sons who weren't a normal lot.
The Nephilim, as they were called, were very nasty guys.
They were super-wicked bullies who believed the devil's lies.

The Bible says that every thought, in nearly every mind,
Was always evil, all the time, and never, never kind.
God was very sad and said, "This sin is out of hand.
I need to send a flood to wipe these people from the land."

So then God said to Noah, "There will be a worldwide flood."
But I will save your family and some creatures from the mud.
Build an ark from gopher wood. Start lopping trees today.
You must build this massive ship exactly as I say."

"Make it three hundred cubits long and fifty cubits wide,
And don't forget to cover it with pitch on every side.
Build it thirty cubits high — that's more than big enough
For you and all the animals, and lots of other stuff."

"Inside this ocean liner make three decks to house my creatures.
A window all along the top will be one of its features."
This type of boat would keep rain out — so it would never sink,
But maybe some ran down through pipes for animals to drink.

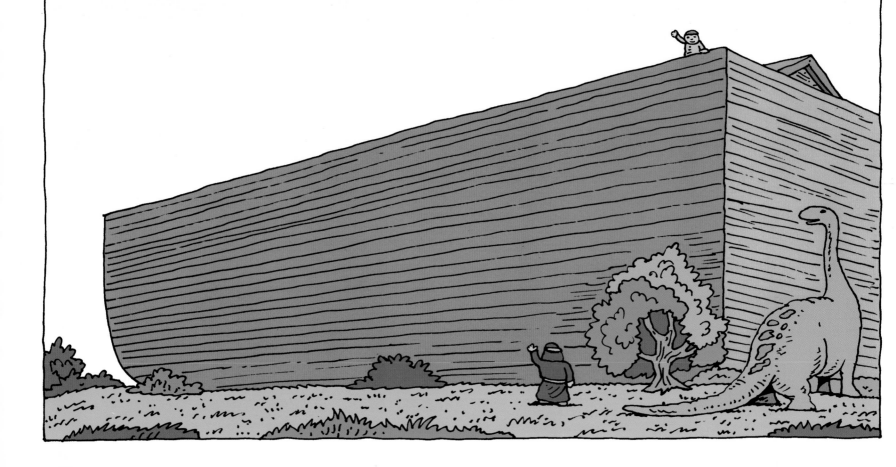

So Noah and his family did exactly what God said,
But people joked and said, "You guys are crazy in the head!"
All the neighbors teased them. They came to point and laugh.
They didn't think that God would ever give the earth a bath.

Noah warned them, "If you want to live through this event,
You'll need to get into my boat. You can't stay in your tent.
The ark will be the only way to stay dry on the day
That God will send the water to wash this world away!"

But nobody would listen, so Noah and his brood
Got busy growing extra crops to stock up lots of food
To fill the troughs at feeding time each day upon the ark.
There'd be no hungry tummies on this floating animal park.

When the ark was finished, God sent animals by their kind.
They all got sent by God, so not one kind got left behind.
Most arrived in pairs, but some came seven at a time.
I'm sure that as they climbed aboard, they formed a formal line.

Now you might be wondering how Noah found a way
To fit in every sort of creature found on earth today.
To answer that, it really helps to bring up an example
That demonstrates how the space inside the ark was ample.

For Noah didn't need to take each sort of dog there is,
Like long haired-dogs, and short-haired dogs, and dogs whose hair is frizz.
He only needed two dogs, and from those two dogs on the ark,
Have come all the dogs we see today — that dig and howl and bark.

And what about the dinosaurs? How did they fit them in?
Did they put them all on diets to make them super-thin?
Well, dinosaurs were babies once, and God most likely chose
Young dinosaurs that were about as high as Noah's nose.

Now, it's not exactly clear what the
ark was like inside,
But we know that it had lots of rooms,
and heaps of space to hide
All the food and goodies that they needed,
and yet more . . .
Once the flood began, they couldn't
pop down to the store.

We know the ark had pens to house beasts of every kind,
And maybe slotted floors to catch what comes out from behind!
I'm guessing they invented an automatic feeding thing
That dropped the food down into pens when Noah pulled a string.

Once on board, the passengers listened to the sound
Of water falling from the sky and bursting from the ground.
God Himself had shut the door and made it waterproof.
No water came in from the door, and none in from the roof.

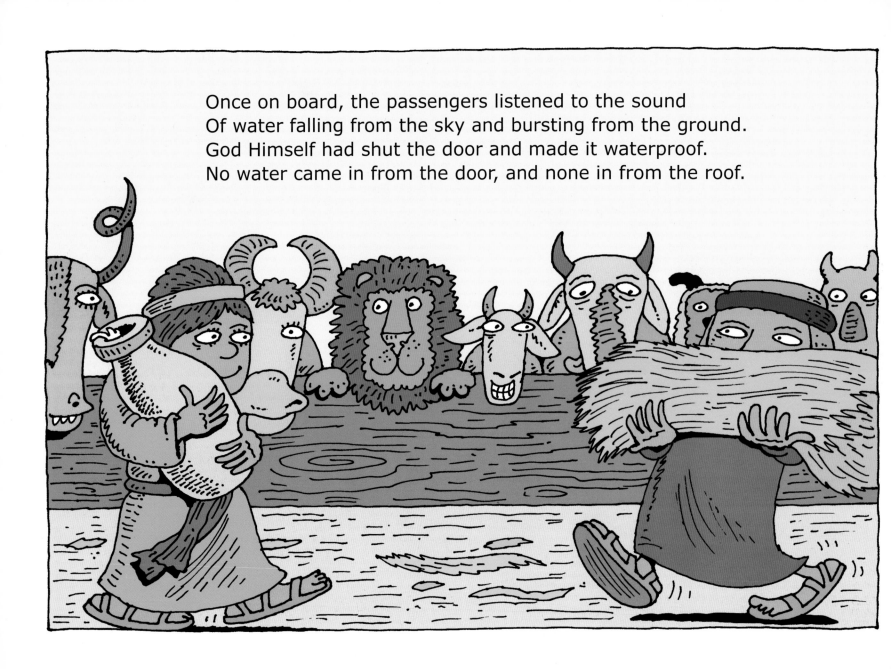

As the water filled the earth, the ark began to float.
Everybody outside wished they'd been on board the boat.
The water rose so high it covered every bit of land,
And underneath the water was swirling mud and sand.
Heaps of stuff got buried as that mud slid all around.
That's why we can dig them up as fossils from the ground.

And way down in the water, all the fish were keeping busy
Swimming in the currents,
    which were making them quite dizzy.
Everything was moving —
    from the ground came water fountains.
It rained for 40 days and nights and covered all
    the mountains.

When the water got so high it couldn't get much worse,
God stopped the rain, and pulled the plug,
  and threw it in reverse.
Pushing up the mountains helped the water drain away.
It carved the rocks and shaped the ground
  that we can see today.

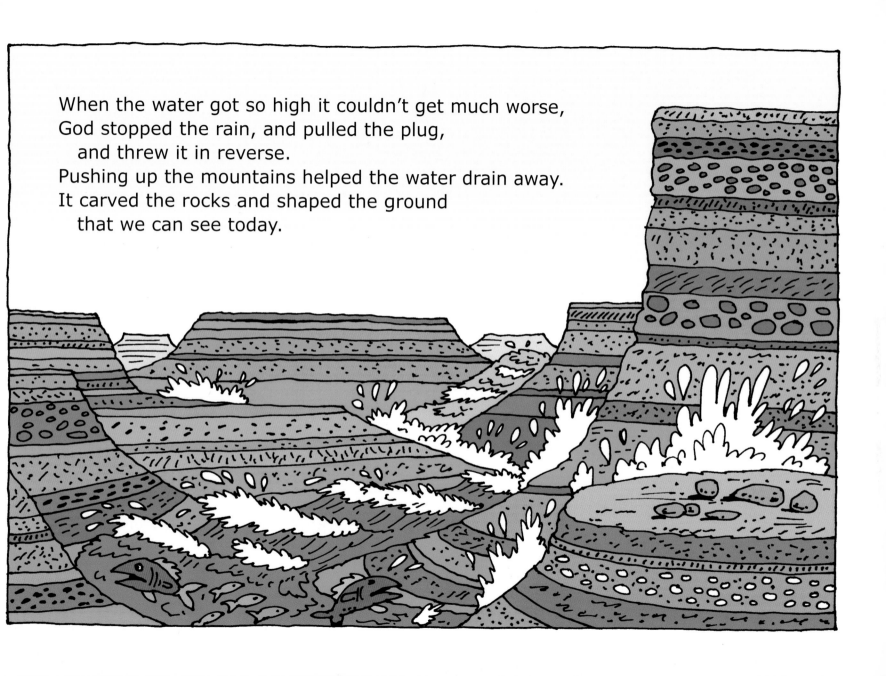

Then one day, inside the ark, when Shem was with the parrots,
And Ham was feeding horses, and Japheth peeling carrots,
Shem's wife called out, "Hey, this ark is getting really jerky!"
And with a bump it landed on a mountaintop near Turkey.

They all knew they couldn't leave until God dried the land.
So with that in mind, Noah took a raven in his hand.
He let it out the window, but that bird just flew around.
It was happy to keep flying till it found a piece of ground.

Then Noah took a pretty dove and did another test,
To find out if the little bird would find a spot to rest.
At first it just came back again, but to his great relief,
The next time Noah sent it out, it came back with a leaf.

After many days afloat, when Noah was six-hundred-and-one,
God explained to Noah that the day had finally come
For his family and the animals to leave the wooden ark,
And on a journey out into the new world to embark.

So everyone was glad to help the animals get out.
They were blinking in the sunlight as they slowly walked about.
And Noah was so thankful that his feet were on dry ground,
He made a sacrifice to God for landing safe and sound.

Then suddenly, they all looked up
  and saw an awesome sight.
A rainbow stretched across the sky,
  colorful and bright.
God said, "There is a message
  in every rainbow that you see —
That was the only worldwide flood
  that there will ever be."

Later on, I'm sure they planned a great big family feast
To celebrate their landing in what we call the Middle East.
"Where will we live?" all the animals then began to wonder.
The kangaroos didn't stick around, but headed for Down Under.

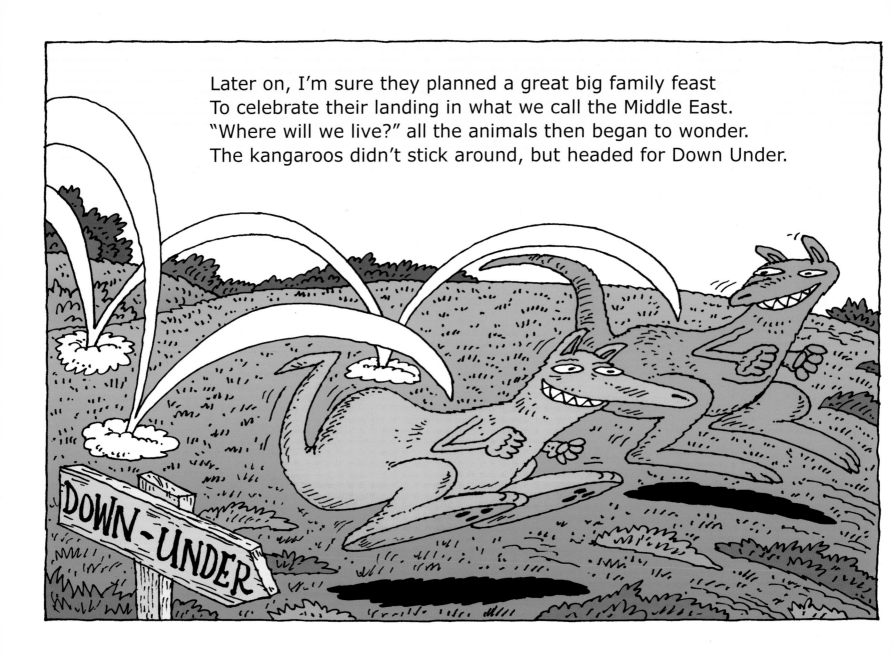

And every single person who lives on earth today
Came from Noah's family who left the ark that day.
God's promise not to flood the world, He will never break,
But the Bible makes it clear that we have something to escape.

Because of sin, this broken world will one day pass away.
It will be pretty scary for those people on that day.
We don't have an ark to build. God has a different plan.
This time we will be saved through the life of just one Man.

Only Jesus has the power to rescue us from sin.
He'll take you up to heaven if you give your life to Him.
But, like Noah, you need to be brave until the day
Jesus comes to take you to His home so far away.

Don't listen to the people who say this isn't true.
It is written in the Bible, so it's straight from God to you.
Trust in Jesus all your life, and make Him your best friend,
For all those who believe in Him there's life that doesn't end.